. . . *for parents and teachers*

The loss of a loved one produces tremendous emotional stress. Whether caused by death, divorce, separation, or other factors, the emotional impact is overwhelming. How a child mourns such a loss is quite important and has great influence on future behavior.

Following an initial feeling of loss and despair, there is a feeling of anger over having been abandoned. An intense fear of investing one's feelings in a new relationship may develop — the fear that the new loved one may desert us, too. Only after this period of adjustment is a child willing to risk love again.

My New Mom and Me provides a touching and tender account of a young girl's painful experience in dealing with the death of her mother. The story is skillfully written and will provide much impetus for thought and discussion. The more children are able to verbalize their feelings, the greater their chances of effectively coping. I encourage parents and teachers to incorporate this story into family or classroom activities to help in this coping process.

MANUEL S. SILVERMAN, Ph.D.
ASSOCIATE PROFESSOR
DEPARTMENT OF GUIDANCE AND
    COUNSELING
LOYOLA UNIVERSITY OF CHICAGO

Betty Ren Wright is the author of over forty books for children. She lives in Wisconsin.

Copyright © 1981, Raintree Publishers Inc.

Library of Congress Number: 80-25529

6 7 8 9 10   89 88 87 86

Printed in the United States of America

Library of Congress Cataloging in Publication Data

Wright, Betty Ren.
  My new mom and me.

  SUMMARY: After her widowed father remarries, a young girl's cat helps her make a few important discoveries about herself.
  [1. Remarriage — Fiction.] I. Day, Betsy.
II. Title.
PZ7.W933Mz   [Fic]   80-25529
ISBN 0-8172-1368-6 lib. bdg.

MY
NEW MOM
AND ME

by Betty Ren Wright

illustrated by Betsy Day

introduction by Manuel S. Silverman, Ph.D.

RAINTREE CHILDRENS BOOKS

Cat is my oldest friend. I like to think
that he remembers all my good times and
bad times.

He remembers a time two summers ago,
when my mom got sick and died. That
was the worst time of all.

I remember the funeral. After it was over, I ran into her bedroom and threw her best perfume on the floor.

Dad held me close. "Try not to be angry," he said. "She didn't want to leave us."

I knew he was right. But sometimes I thought, *If she knew how sad I was going to be, she would have found a way to stay alive.*

Cat was sad too. He had been Mom's special pet. After she died, he walked from room to room, trying to find her. When we watched TV at night, he sat and stared at us. When Dad called to him, he ran away.

"Poor Cat," Dad said.

"He's smart," I said. "He doesn't want
to love us, because he's afraid we might die
too."

"Soon he'll learn to feel safe with us,"
said Dad. "You'll see."

Cat wouldn't always come when we
called him, but he would curl up on my
bed each night. I would tell him how
lonely I was. Sometimes I cried.

Then, last summer, I told him that Dad was going to get married again. Cat didn't like it any better than I did.

Dad had long talks with me about his
new wife. "We'll have fun together," he
said. "You're going to love Elena."

But I knew I wouldn't. *We don't need
her*, I thought. Dad looked so happy,
though, that I just couldn't tell him that.

The first day that Elena came to our apartment to live, she tried to hug me. I wouldn't let her.

Cat felt just the same. If Elena put out her hand to him, he ran off. If she dropped a piece of cheese in his dish, he waited for her to go away before he ate it.

Sometimes Elena would look at me and
at Cat and then at me again. Her smile
would fade away. I wondered if she was
sorry she had come to live with us. I
almost hoped she was.

One night, Dad had to go out of town
on business. Elena and I were alone.

After dinner I stayed in my room and
thought about how different everything
was. I wished I could run into the living
room and find Mom sitting there, as if
nothing had happened.

Then I heard Cat mewing loudly.

He sounded terribly scared. I couldn't
tell where he was.

I looked under my bed and opened all
the dresser drawers. I looked behind the
desk, and I opened the closet door. He
sounded much closer, but he wasn't in the
closet.

"Elena!" I cried. "Something's happened
to Cat!"

21

Elena ran into my room and crowded
into the closet with me.

"Meeeeowww," howled Cat.

Elena listened carefully. "He must be
down inside the wall," she said.

As soon as she said that, I remembered
the loose board at the back of my closet
shelf. For weeks I had been meaning to ask
Dad to fix it.

I showed Elena the shelf. She pushed
aside some boxes and uncovered a hole.
The board had fallen off.

"That's it," said Elena. "Cat slipped
through the hole and fell behind the wall.
Can you find a hammer? And maybe a pair
of gloves too?"

I ran to Dad's workbench and got the
hammer and gardening gloves.

Elena used the hammer to give a hard
whack to the closet wall. Again and again
she hit it, until the wallboard shattered.

Cat howled in fright.

Elena put on the gloves and pulled on
the broken boards. The boards cracked and
split to the floor. She reached into the
opening.

"He'll scratch you," I warned.

"Poor Cat," Elena whispered. She rocked back on her heels and waited. "Come, Cat, come, Cat," she sang.

His head came into the opening. There was dust on his ears and a wild look in his eyes. He stopped when he saw Elena, and then, when she put out her arms, he jumped into them.

I was so glad to have him back that I couldn't say anything at first. Finally I said, "We made kind of a mess of the closet, didn't we?"

I looked at Elena — really looked at her for the first time. "Thank you for helping Cat," I said.

We went outside and sat together on the back porch steps. Elena petted Cat and sang to him. After a while, he pushed his head into the warm place under her arm.

"That's what he used to do to my mom," I said. I didn't mean to tell her that, but it slipped out.

Elena nodded. "Your mother taught Cat how to love," she said. "He'll never forget her, but maybe he's tired of keeping all that love locked inside."

We sat for a while, just thinking and listening to Cat purr. It was the first purr I had heard in a very long time.

Then she put her arm around me, and I leaned against her. It felt good — better than I had expected.